To Life. To Love. To You.

-Denise & Andy

**www.mascotbooks.com**

*Soap on a Rope*

**For more information, please contact:**
Mascot Books
560 Herndon Parkway #120
Herndon, VA 20170

info@mascotbooks.com

Library of Congress Control Number: 2014919946

CPSIA Code: PRT0115A
ISBN-13: 978-1-63177-034-0

Printed in the United States

# SOAP on a Rope

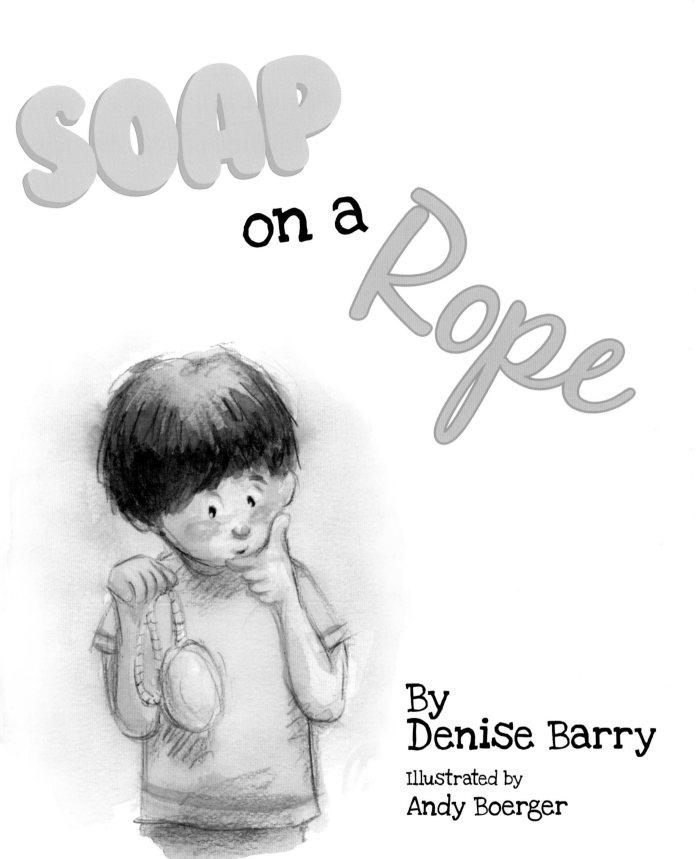

By
Denise Barry

Illustrated by
Andy Boerger

The Silvas

1572

2

A sparkly red box arrived in the mail.
Tied with ribbons, it said, "To Abigail".
Abigail jumped up and down with joy.
What was inside? She hoped for a toy.

Her dog, Foo Man Chew, hoped for a bone,
But he'd settle quite nicely for an ice cream cone.
They ran in the house at the speed of light.
The colorful ribbons danced around like a kite.

"Hey, Nolan, come quick, I have a surprise.
I want you to see this, so open your eyes!"
Her brother came running, "Abby, what could it be?
Do you think it's a monkey? Let's open it and see!"

They tore off the wrapping and peeked inside.
Abby's heart did a flip and her eyes got real wide.
It wasn't a toy. It was a big bar of soap,
And not just some soap, but some soap on a rope!

Why would someone give her this horrible thing,
A big wad of cleanser with a long piece of string?
Did she smell really bad, from her head to her toes?
Was this a mean joke? She wanted to know!

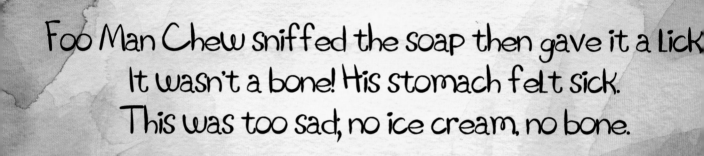

Foo Man Chew sniffed the soap then gave it a lick.
It wasn't a bone! His stomach felt sick.
This was too sad, no ice cream, no bone.

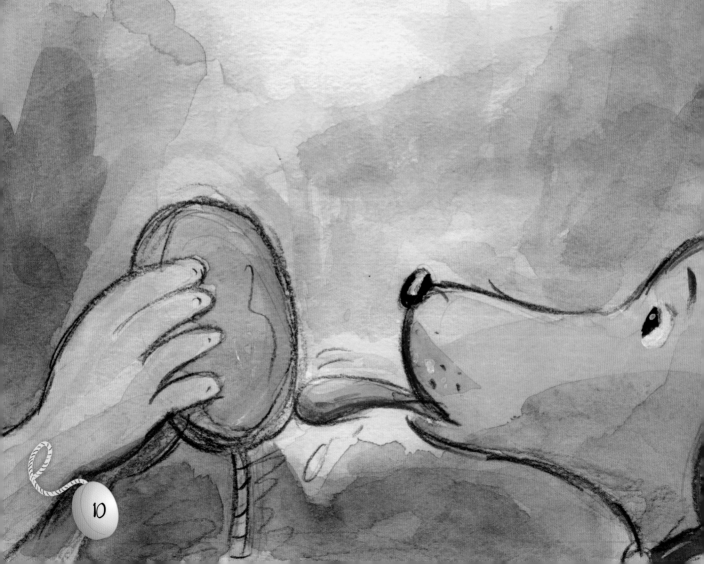

He thought about leaving to find a new home.

"What's going on, Abby? Why are you sad?
Do you think that your gift is really so bad?"
"Oh Nolan, it's awful! What do you think?"
She handed it over and cried, "Do I stink?!"

Nolan could not resist, "Well, yes, yes, you do!
But maybe you're not thinking this all the way through
It looks like a bar of soap on a string,
But nothing is ever only one thing!"

"There has to be something fun we can do...
I've got an idea! Follow me, you two!"

15

They ran to the yard
and straight up a hill.
Foo Man Chew was still sad,
but he liked a good thrill.
"Watch what I do, Abby,
then when I'm done
You grab the hose
and we'll have us some fun!"

What was Nolan doing? He was dragging the soap
To the top of the hill then back down by its rope.
Was he losing his marbles? Abby thought, Yes.
But it was kind of exciting, she had to confess.

19

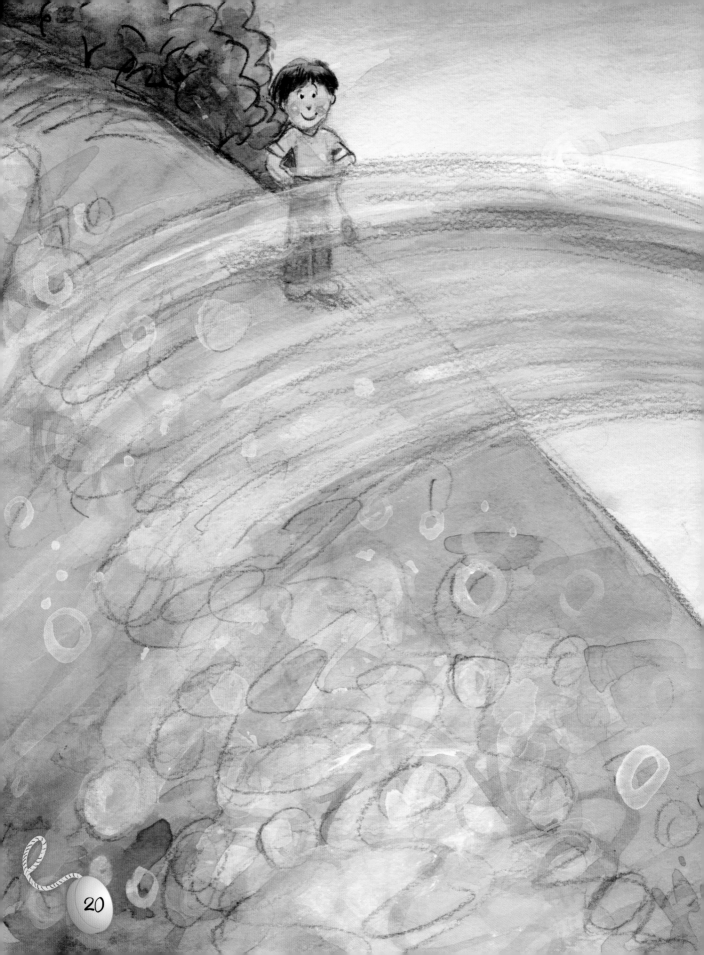

"It's your turn now, Abby, spray the hose at the soap!"
So she sprayed the array all along the steep slope.
An explosion of bubbles came up from the ground.
A caboodle of them, all floating around.
Abigail shouted with a big burst of air,
"I can't believe we made this, just look at it here!"

They raced to the top of the hill and plopped down
Then pushed themselves forward and slid all around.
It felt like a car wash, but without the car,
Or a big, sudsy bath. It was so bizarre!

Foo Man Chew didn't know if he wanted to play.
Wasn't he supposed to be running away?
Nobody loved him or he'd have a nice bone.

Okay, just one slide,
and then he'd leave home.

25

Bubbles look empty as they float through the air
But guess what's inside as they soar everywhere?
The musical sounds that happy kids make.
See all the notes? Those bubbles will break!

When the bubbles burst open, out poured a song
Which was heard by all children from here to Hong Kong.

Come and play, come and play, we are waiting for you.
It's Abby and Nolan and our dog, Foo Man Chew.
Bring a swim suit with you...
And a dog bone or two!

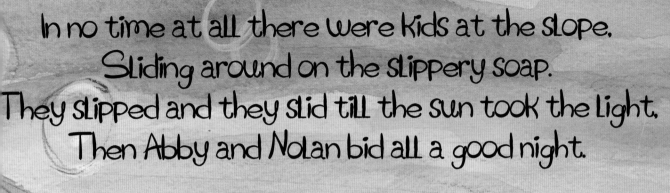

In no time at all there were kids at the slope,
Sliding around on the slippery soap.
They slipped and they slid till the sun took the light,
Then Abby and Nolan bid all a good night.

Later that night, all cozy in bed
Visions of bubbles filled Abigail's head.
Something felt wrong though, what could it be?
Her eyes popped wide open, "Oh no, oh dear me!"

She threw on her robe and raced outside.
"My soap on a rope! Where is it?" she cried.
"Please let it be there, not melted away.
I'm sorry for thinking it was goofy today!"

There it was, by the hill, quite mushy and small.
Abby picked it up gently, not caring at all.

"Thank goodness you're fine because now I can see
What a wonderful gift you were to me.
I had wished for a toy but saw you and lost hope.
But you're not just some soap, you're my soap on a rope!"

33

Denise Barry is the author of the children's picture book, *What Does the Tooth Fairy Do with Our Teeth?* and the upcoming middle grade book *Sweeney Mack and the Slurp and Burp Competition.* She is also an inspirational writer whose work has been featured on various websites and in the best-selling book, *Watch Her Thrive: Stories of Hope, Courage and Strength.* Denise lives in Buffalo, NY with her husband and two children.

www.denisebarry.net